Cowgirl Kate and Cocoa

Horse in the House

Cowgirl Kate and Cocoa

Horse in the House

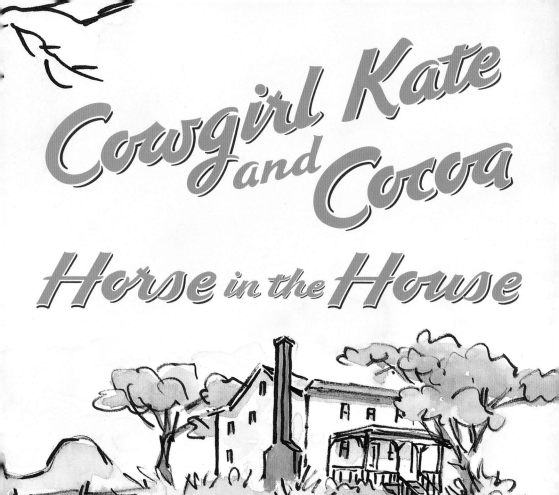

Written by **Erica Silverman**

Painted by **Betsy Lewin**

ʃ sandpiper

Houghton Mifflin Harcourt

Boston   New York

To Ralph, in loving memory—E.S.
To Erica—B.L.

Text copyright © 2009 by Erica Silverman
Illustrations copyright © 2009 by Betsy Lewin

www.hmhbooks.com

The text of this book is set in Filosofia.
The illustrations in this book were done in watercolors
on Strathmore one-ply Bristol paper.
The display type was hand-lettered by Georgia Deaver.

The Library of Congress has cataloged the hardcover edition as follows:
Silverman, Erica.
Cowgirl Kate and Cocoa: horse in the house/written by Erica Silverman; painted by Betsy Lewin.
p. cm.
Summary: When Cocoa decides to explore the house, Cowgirl Kate has a hard time convincing him he
must return to the barn.
[1. Horses—Fiction. 2. Cowgirls—Fiction. 3. Dwellings—Fiction.] I. Lewin, Betsy, ill. II. Title.
PZ7.S58625Cof   2009
[E]—dc22   2007043356

ISBN 978-0-15-205390-1
ISBN 978-0-547-31672-7 pb

Manufactured in China
LEO 10 9 8 7 6 5 4 3 2 1
4500207025

Chapter 1
A Small Stall

Cowgirl Kate felt horse whiskers on her face.

She woke up.

She opened her eyes.

"Cocoa!" she said.

"How did you get into the house?"

Cocoa grinned.

"I pushed the door open
and walked in," he said.

"You have to leave!" cried Cowgirl Kate.

"What if my parents see you?"

"They won't," said Cocoa.

"I saw them drive off in the truck."

"They'll be back," said Cowgirl Kate.

She jumped out of bed.

She got dressed.

"Come on," she said.

"I'll walk you back to the barn."

"I'm tired of the barn," said Cocoa.

"And I've always wanted to explore
the house."

He looked under the bed.

"Where's your hay?" he asked.

"Cocoa," said Cowgirl Kate,

"you have looked in my window many times.

Have you ever seen any hay?"

"I thought you were hiding it," said Cocoa.
He sniffed the rug.

He looked behind the dresser.

Then he snorted.

"No hay!

What kind of stall *is* this?"

"It's a bedroom," said Cowgirl Kate.

"People sleep in bedrooms.

Horses belong in barns."

"I belong with you," said Cocoa.

"But your stall is too small."

He turned and walked out.

"Where are you going?" asked Cowgirl Kate.

"To find a bigger stall," said Cocoa.

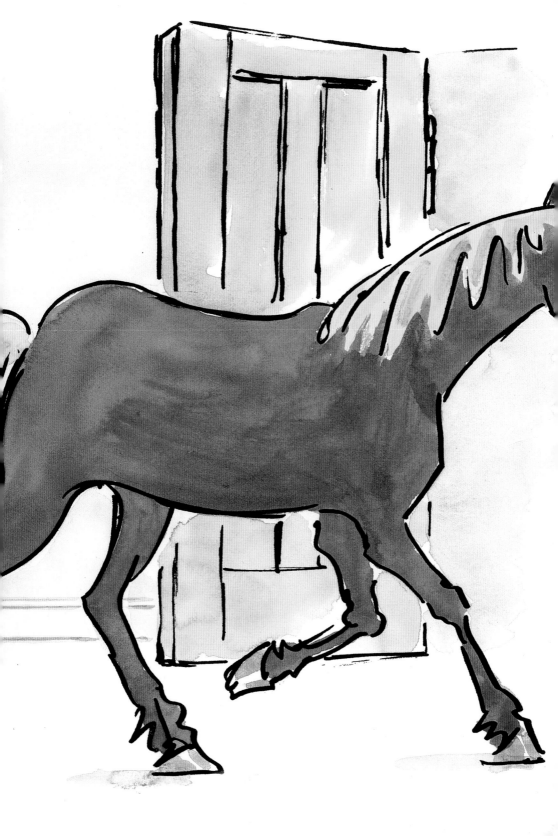

Chapter 2

An Even Smaller Stall

"Cocoa, wait!" said Cowgirl Kate.

"I will show you the house."

"Yippee!" cried Cocoa.

"But then you must leave," she said.

"Horseflies!" grumbled Cocoa.

He nudged a door open and walked in.

"This stall is smaller than yours," he said.

"It's called a bathroom," said Cowgirl Kate.

"This bin would not hold many oats," said Cocoa.

"It's a sink," said Cowgirl Kate.

She turned on the faucet.

"The water moves too fast!" said Cocoa.

He looked around.

"What's this?" he asked.

"A toilet," said Cowgirl Kate.

And she flushed it.

"I do not like water that swirls," said Cocoa.

Suddenly, his eyes grew wide.

"You could put lots of oats in that bin!"

"It's a bathtub," said Cowgirl Kate.
"It's where people take baths."
"Oats are better than baths!"
 said Cocoa.
"There are oats in the barn,"
 said Cowgirl Kate.
"There must be oats in the house,
 too," said Cocoa.
 He headed down the hall.
"I will find a nice, big stall," he said.
"And then I will find the oats."

Chapter 3
The Biggest Stall

Cocoa walked into the living room.

"Look!" he cried.

"Horses *do* belong in houses!"

"Those are not real horses," said Cowgirl Kate.

"Those are horse statues."

Cocoa raised his head high.

"Real horses are better than statues," he said.

"Every house should have a real horse."

"I don't think my parents will agree,"

said Cowgirl Kate.

Cocoa flicked his tail.

Magazines flew off the table.

He swung his head.

A lamp fell over.

"That's it," cried Cowgirl Kate.

"You're going back to the barn right now!"

Cocoa stomped his hooves.

"The barn is boring," he said.

"I am never going back to the barn!"

Cocoa looked around the living room.
"This stall is nice and big," he said.
"Maybe I will live here."
Suddenly, he spotted a basket of fruit.
"Yum!" he said.
And he hurried to the dining room table.

CHOMP!

He bit into an apple.

"Yuck!" he said.

"This apple tastes funny."

"It's made of wax," said Cowgirl Kate.
Cocoa snorted.
"You have fake horses
  and fake apples," he said.
"But I am a real horse.
  And I need real food."

Cowgirl Kate sighed.

"Real horses live in *barns*," she said.

"Not this horse," said Cocoa.

"Not anymore!"

Chapter 4
The Best Stall of All

"I will give you a snack," said Cowgirl Kate.

"I would like a snack," said Cocoa.

"But then," said Cowgirl Kate,

"you must promise to go back to the barn."

"Do I have to?" asked Cocoa.

Cowgirl Kate nodded. "Promise?"

"I promise," said Cocoa.

"Okay, follow me," said Cowgirl Kate.

Cowgirl Kate led Cocoa into the kitchen.
She opened the refrigerator door.
"Yeehaw!" cried Cocoa. "A giant bin.
And it's filled with food."
"It's called a refrigerator,"
said Cowgirl Kate.
"Refrigerator," Cocoa repeated.
He gazed at all the food.
He smacked his lips.

head.

he said.

e soon."

e," said Cocoa.

d Cowgirl Kate.

id Cocoa.

aid Cowgirl Kate.

"Do you want an apple or a carrot?"
asked Cowgirl Kate.
"Yes, please," said Cocoa.
Cowgirl Kate smiled.
She gave him an apple and a carrot.
Then she gave him another apple and
another carrot.

Cowgirl Kate shook he
"You must leave now,"
"My parents will be hon
"But I don't want to lea
"But you promised," sa
"But I love the house,"
"Well, I love the barn,"

Cocoa snorted.

"What's so great about the barn?" he asked.

"Come on," said Cowgirl Kate.

"I will show you."

Cocoa took one last look around the kitchen.

He nuzzled the refrigerator.

He sighed.

"Cocoa, hurry!" said Cowgirl Kate.

"My parents are coming!"

Chapter 5

The Barn

Cowgirl Kate led Cocoa to the barn.

"It's just a barn," said Cocoa.

"What is there to love?"

Cowgirl Kate pointed.
"I love how the sunlight comes in
through the cracks in the wall," she said.
Cocoa looked.
"That is nice," he said.

Cowgirl Kate inhaled deeply.
"And I love the smell of saddle leather
and fresh hay," she said.
Cocoa sniffed.
"That is a good smell," he said.

"And I love
the sound of all the horses
snorting and stomping, nickering
and neighing," said Cowgirl Kate.
Cocoa perked up his ears.
"Me, too," he agreed.

Cowgirl Kate stroked Cocoa's neck.
"But what I love best about the barn,"
she said, "is you."
Cocoa thought for a moment.
Then he said, "It's true. The barn would
not be the same without me."
"Exactly!" said Cowgirl Kate.

"Okay. I will live in the barn," said Cocoa.

"But I will visit the house, too."

Cowgirl Kate sighed.

"Do you have to?" she asked.

"Yes," said Cocoa.

"The barn is my home, but there are two
things in the house that I love."

"What are they?" asked Cowgirl Kate.

"You," said Cocoa.

"And the refrigerator."

"This is the best stall in the house!"
said Cocoa.
"This is where I will live!"

Cowgirl Kate shook her head.

"You must leave now," she said.

"My parents will be home soon."

"But I don't want to leave," said Cocoa.

"But you promised," said Cowgirl Kate.

"But I love the house," said Cocoa.

"Well, I love the barn," said Cowgirl Kate.

"Do you want an apple or a carrot?"
asked Cowgirl Kate.
"Yes, please," said Cocoa.
Cowgirl Kate smiled.
She gave him an apple and a carrot.
Then she gave him another apple and
another carrot.